som
t hee

This book is dedicated to
young students everywhere

WALKER BOOKS
AND SUBSIDIARIES
LONDON · BOSTON · SYDNEY · AUCKLAND

First published in Great Britain 2008 by Walker Books Ltd
87 Vauxhall Walk, London SE11 5HJ

First published in the United States 2007 by Hyperion Books for Children.
British Publication Rights arranged with Sheldon Fogelman Agency, Inc.

10 9 8 7 6 5

© 2007 Mo Willems

The right of Mo Willems to be identified as author/illustrator of this work
has been asserted by him in accordance with the Copyright, Designs and
Patents Act 1988

This book has been typeset in Coup Light and Village-Roman.

Printed in China

British Library Cataloguing in Publication Data:
a catalogue record for this book is available from the British Library

ISBN 978-1-4063-1382-6

www.walkerbooks.co.uk

Knuffle Bunny Too

A CASE OF MISTAKEN IDENTITY BY Mo Willems

One morning, not so long ago,
Trixie took a walk with her daddy.

By now Trixie really
knew how to talk.

...then I'll show Margot, and then I'll show Jane, and then I'll show Leela, and then I'll show Rebecca, and then I'll show Noah, and then I'll show Robbie, and then I'll show Toshi, and then I'll show Casey, and then I'll show Conny, and then I'll show Parker, and then I'll show Brian, and then...

And talk and talk.

Trixie was excited because she was taking her one-of-a-kind Knuffle Bunny somewhere very special ...

school!

Trixie couldn't wait to show Knuffle Bunny to Ms Greengrove and all her classmates.

But, as her daddy was kissing her goodbye, Trixie saw Sonja.

Suddenly Trixie's one-of-a-kind
Knuffle Bunny wasn't so
one-of-a-kind any more.

The morning did not go well.

The afternoon was worse.

When the bell rang, Ms Greengrove
returned the Knuffle Bunnies.

And the day got better.

Then, before she knew it,

it was time to go home

Trixie "ate" her dinner,

devoured her
dessert,

brushed her
teeth ...

and tried to escape the Mummy and Daddy robots from Planet Snurp!

At half-past bedtime, Trixie was tucked in,

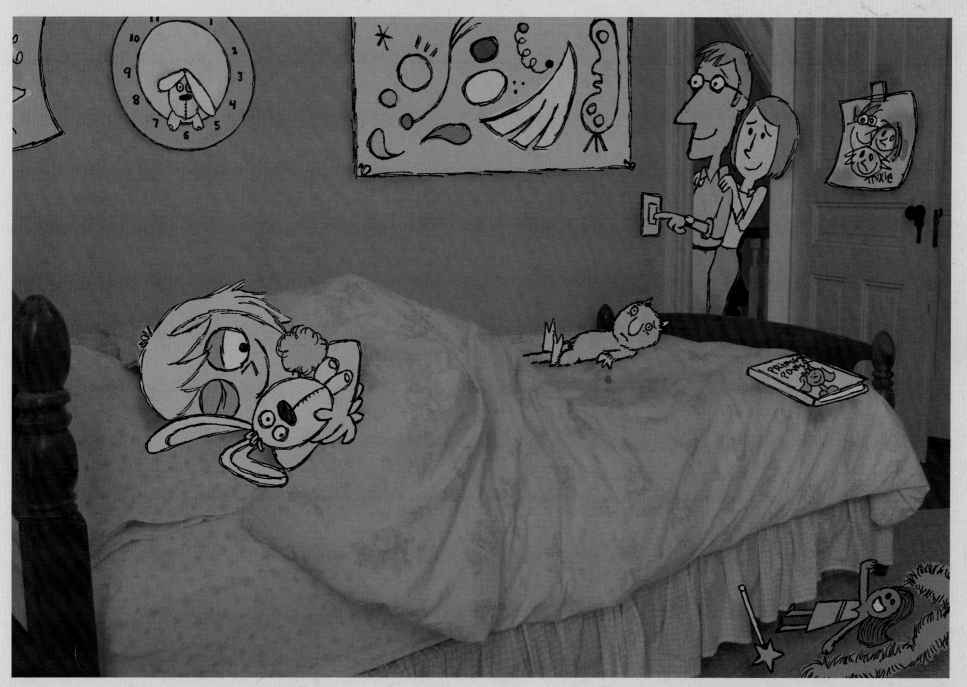

ready to go to sleep.

But a few hours later ...

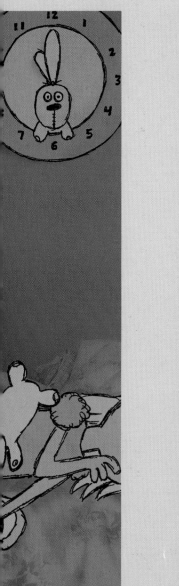

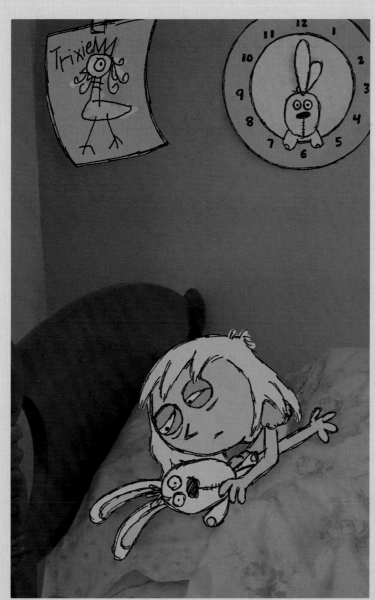

something.

Trixie marched into her
mummy and daddy's
room and said,

Trixie's daddy tried to explain what "2.30 a.m." meant.

He asked, "Can we deal with this
in the morning?"

Trixie's daddy went to the phone.

Before he had even made it
down the stairs,

the phone rang.

replied Trixie's daddy.

Arrangements were made.

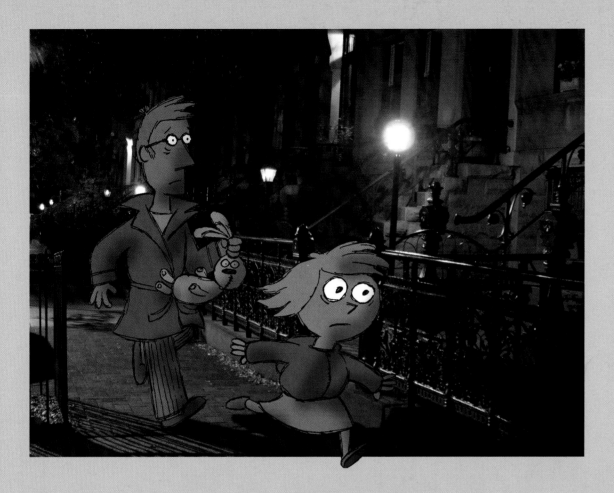

Trixie and her daddy rushed
across the neighbourhood!

Trixie did not
want to be late.

Neither did Sonja.

There was an exchange.

And the Knuffle Bunnies were back

where they belonged.

said Sonja.

Trixie replied.

Then they both said,

I'm glad you've got your bunny back!

at the **exact**

same

time!

And that's how Trixie found her first* best friend.

*Apart from Knuffle Bunny, of course.

Special thanks to the real Trixie and her mummy, Tom Drysdale, the Brooklyn Public Library, the Robinson family, the Lewine family, Ms Theope, Ms Holton and the PS107 community.

EPILOGUE

The next morning both Trixie and Sonja rushed to school.

The new best friends had a lot of catching up to do.